# *Worldwide* Food Court

Bobby Cinema

**Bonus:
Bobby Cinema movie plot
summaries and ideas**

authorHOUSE®

AuthorHouse™
1663 Liberty Drive
Bloomington, IN 47403
www.authorhouse.com
Phone: 1 (800) 839-8640

Published by AuthorHouse    03/11/2016

ISBN: 978-1-5049-8487-4 (sc)
ISBN: 978-1-5049-8486-7 (e)

Print information available on the last page.

Any people depicted in stock imagery provided
by Thinkstock are models, and such images are
being used for illustrative purposes only.
Certain stock imagery © Thinkstock.

This book is printed on acid-free paper.

Because of the dynamic nature of the Internet, any web
addresses or links contained in this book may have changed
since publication and may no longer be valid. The views
expressed in this work are solely those of the author and do
not necessarily reflect the views of the publisher, and the
publisher hereby disclaims any responsibility for them.

# Contents

## Bobby Cinema Movie Plot Summary and Ideas

# Contents

## Plot Summary:

Little Indian boy, about five years old and her big sister, goes to a shopping mall in Dallas, TX. The boy's name is Naveen and sister Lekha, and their are shopping with their mother, Susmita, who is making a call. Naveen and Susmita has a very active imagination, and when the three go to the food court for lunch, he begins to let his imagination run wild. While Lekha takes him around the food court to figure out what he wants for lunch, Naveen experiences an exciting trip around the world.

Naveen, his mother, Susmita, and his big sister, Lekha, enter the mall Dallas Mall. Susmita has come to the mall to buy a new dress for a party for Naveen's dad, Sai. As they go inside the mall, Naveen looks around.

As they walk into the mall, Naveen grabs hold of Lekha's hand, and Lekha tells him, "Welcome to the Dallas Mall. It's a lot different on the outside, but it's really beautiful when you go inside. There are a million stores and food courts in here."

Naveen asks her, "What is a food court?"

Lekha tells him, "They are places where they sell all kinds of food that we could possiblywant to eat. Each restaurant there sells a different kind of food. It's like going to Disney's Epcot Center and looking at all the different countries. I think I threw up in the UK once."

Naveen responses, "Wow. It's like walking around the world."

Lekha tells Naveen, "Tell me about it. We could check out America's favorite restaurant called B&W restaurant."

Before they leave, Lekha tells Susmita, "Excuse me mom, I wanted to ask if we could go to the food court for a minute."

Susmita gets off her phone and tells Lekha, "Sure, I'm kind of hungry too." While they head to the food court, Naveen sees all the different kinds of stores on the way there.

One of them is a music store, and he imagines that he sees Mozart playing on a piano in the window. Another is a movie theatre, and he imagines that the people are actually buying tickets for a shuttle ride to the moon. One of the shops they pass is Penny's, and Naveen imagines that it is a mint, where people are minting coins.

When they reach the food court, Susmita tells Lekha, "Alright, Naveen, you can pick anything you want. And Lekha Promise to look after him. And would you get me a soda?"

Lekha tells Susmita, "Yes mom, no problem." Lekha and Naveen then head into the food court while Susmita sits down in a chair, and continues talking to Sai on the phone.

They can see B&W restaurant on the other side of the food court, but there are many other restaurants on the way. The first one they see is called Chicken Heaven. Naveen looks in and sees chickens delivering chicken feed to the customers. They are also delivering corn, potatoes, and eggs. "Just like being on a farm," he tells Lekha.

Then they pass the Chinese restaurant, Wong Palace. Naveen sees Chinese men cutting noodles with swords, and cutting lettuce with Sais. Then a samurai flips over the counter, where a food tray was tossed to the side. The samurai catches it and puts it on the counter, and says to a customer, "That's 5 yen, please."

Next they walk over to a British restaurant, Neville's Castle, where a royal butler with a big hat and long coat serves people fish and chips.

Lekha tells Naveen, "Most people don't know that chips are actually French fries. British call them chips."

Naveen says loud, "Yes, Heard they are delicious."

The butler tells the customer, "How many orders of fish and chips do you want, sir?" The customer tells him, "Three, please."

The butler tells the cook, "We've got order for three fish and chips. And get them a cup of English tea with lemon and scones."

Naveen and Lekha, pass another restaurant, and they see it is a cookie shop, Al's Cookies. They see cook taking gingerbread cookies out of the oven, and the cookies are singing "Do You Know the Muffin Man." The cook tells them, "These cookies are very entertaining and delicious."

The gingerbread man ask, "Any other requests?"

The cook tells them, "Yeah, do you know the song any One Direction?"

The gingerbread men, "I don't know the song, but if you hum a few bars, we'll try to wing it." Naveen is amused by cookies coming alive and entertaining him.

Next stop was an Indian restaurant with picture of Ganesha (elephant god) with laddus in his hand. Lekha tells Naveen "Let us not stop here. Mom makes us eat Indian food every day."

Naveen stops to admire restaurant with Eiffel tower wondering what it was. Lekha explains "Naveen, this is in Paris. I love their fashions." They see a man with chef's hat making crepes like mom making Dosa." Naveen pulls Lekha's hand to signal his sister that that is not his favorite thing to eat.

They only have two restaurants to pass to get to B&W restaurant now. The first is a German restaurant, called Ishmael's Brats. Inside, a German man wearing a traditional German

suit asks a customer, "How many bratwurst and sauerkraut do you want?"

The customer tells him, "Just one of each."

The German man tells the cook, "Hey, Hans! One sauerkraut and one bratwurst! And try not to spill on my Mercedes again, because I had that waxed." They started to move on to next.

The other restaurant is an Italian restaurant, Mario's Pizza. An Italian waiter is singing to the customers and playing an accordion. Another waiter asks a customer, "What can I get you?"

The customer tells him, "One pesto pasta and one pepperoni pizza."

The Italian waiter tells the customer, "Coming right up." He then calls back to the kitchen, "Hey Mario! Hey Luigi! One green pasta and one pizza! And do not spill the food on my Ferrari, I just got it detailed." Then they finally reach the B&W restaurant.

Naveen sees the B&W root beer, and Lekha asks him, "So what'll it be, Naveen?" Naveen tells her, "How about the onion rings, and a B&W root beer."

The waiter arrives, and Naveen imagines him as Uncle Sam as he says, "Howdy ma'am, my name's Uncle Sam, and I'll be your server today. Now tell me, what can Uncle Sam do for you?"

Lekha tells Uncle Sam, "One order of onion rings, and one B&W root beer, and make it a small."

Uncle Sam tells Lekha, "Coming right up. Hey Charlie! Don't forget to wave the red, white, and blue, because we got some onion rings and a B&W root beer. Hey and stay away frommy fireworks, I'll fire them later on America's birthday."

After Lekha grabs the tray with onion rings and the root beer, both of them turn around, and everything is different for Naveen. All of the food court is back to normal, with regular

waiters working the different counters. They make their way back to Susmita and sit down. Susmita tells Sai on the phone, "Okay Sai. We'll be home in an hour." Susmita hangs up the phone and asks Lekha and Naveen, "So, everything went okay? This is a big food court, I hope you guys didn't get lost." Lekha tells Susmita, "No, mom, we didn't get lost. I think we found the place just in time." After they sit down, Naveen eats his onion rings and drinks his root beer. As they exit the mall, Naveen turns around and sees the mall as a big globe of the world. He sees all of the waiters that he had imagined in the food court and he tells himself, "It's like walking around the entire world."

THE END

About Author: Bobby Chavala with pen name Bobby Cinema is an upcoming author published several books both fiction and action stories. His books can be purchased in all major book stores including Amazon.

This is his second children book which is written specially for his niece Lekha and his nephew Naveen.

# Bobby Cinema Movie Plot Summary and Ideas

**Bobby Cinema Movie idea #1:**

**Pitching my movie to Movie Studios**

**Genre: Action and Comedy**

**Ages: 18-35**

**Movie idea:**

**Pen Pal:**

Detective Lieutenant Lex Rutherford is an excellent cop for the Portland Police Department. and high decorated. But blew a drug sting operation that could put away Rico Ramirez a top drug kingpin that Rutherford is been after for two years. His boss Chief Angelo Petrillo was upset with him and chewed him out for a few minutes and considering

suspending him. But Chief Petrillo, gives Rutheford one more chance to get Ramirez. He has one week to bring Ramirez to justice and shut down his operation or he's fired. Rutherford been working alone for eight years on the force, never had a partner because they always hold him back. Besides no one wants to work with him, because he is like Portland's own Dirty Harry. After reading Ramirez file, he had a guy who used to work for him. His name was Andy Wilkins, who used to work in his shipping company. He was arrested and the mastermind of his drug deal and money laundering operation. Portland P.D. found drugs and laundered money in his house and was arrested. He also found a gun that was used to kill Ramirez partner Ramon Ramirez who was his brother. Looking at Wilkins file, maybe his key to bring down Ramirez. He visited him in prison, Wilkins was hostile to Rutherford at first. Because he doesn't trust cops, who put him away in the first place. But Rutherford told him, you can trust me. I'm not like all the other cops here. Wilkins believe him, he told him his

side of the story. That he was set up by Ramirez, he planted the drugs, laundered money and the murder weapon in his house. He was a single parent and his one year daughter watched him be arrested by the cops, was no laughing matter. His daughter is now three lives with his parents and been rotting in this prison for two years, figure out a way to put away Ramirez. But he can't, he has a cop in his payroll and the one who set him up in the first place. Rutheford made a deal with him, he has a friend who is the Governor, who used to work in security once and took a bullet for him and owed him a couple favors. Could give him a temporary release with a new identity and a new job as his new partner on the police force and help him take down Ramirez. If were successful, the Governor will give you a full pardon and a clean record so you can start over and be with your daughter. Wilkins agreed, Rutherford makes the arrangements and give him a new identity Andy Willis who just transferred from N.Y.P.D. assigned him as a new partner. No one knows his identity except Lex. Together their going

to take down Ramirez, they have one week to do it or Rutherford is fired and Wilkins will be back in jail. Can they do it and bring down top Drug Kingpin, I can say they need a miracle for them, god help them.

**Bobby Cinema Movie idea #2:**

**Pitching my movie to Movie Studios**

**Genre: Action and Comedy movie**

**Ages: 18-35**

**Movie idea:**

**Pop Diva:**

Marvin Foreman A highly decorated police officer in the L.A.P.D. who was on the force for seven years. His career is not going anywhere since he failed the detective exam and the sergeant exam a few times. He barely graduated from the academy. He and his partner were taking down a huge drug bust and bringing down their suppliers. His partner got the credit

and he got the promotion as detective. Marvin is still a beat cop, but only works as a celebrity security division. The next celebrity that he has to protect is Pop Diva. A successful pop superstar who is throwing a five day concert in the Staples Center and begin her world tour. Mostly Marvin would never want to protect a pop star like Pop Diva. Because all singers are arrogant, selfish and egotistical. But not Pop Diva, she has a heart of gold that Marvin didn't realize. Until he saved her by an assassin and took out her killer. We found out, this assassin didn't act alone. Somebody hired him to kill her. Now she instant police protection and has to cancel her world tour, until we find out who is trying to kill her. Marvin knows that, those guys will never find out who killed her. The only way he can find out, who hired that assassin, he have to solve this case himself. He has a friend, who can help Diva keep a low profile until we find this guy. Only one place that will never find her, is in Marvin's dorm suite, since he's an Residential Advisor in USC and got a full scholarship here seven years ago before he

went to the academy. The campus is a safe place to stay right now, but sooner or later somebody will look for her and track her down. So, he gets some help from his friend Roy Kelsey who teaches computer programming and has a computer lab in an abandon warehouse that nobody in the college ever uses. It's kind of Roy and Marvin's sanctuary where they can relax once in a while and best place to find out who is trying to kill Diva. Marvin might think it might be the drug kingpin that he tried to bust a week ago. We only got his supplier. I think he was about to make a deal with the D.A. about how he was working for and a suspended sentence if he testify. But his deal will come short, until his boss sent an assassin in the police department to kill him and they're back at square one. You think Marvin can find this drug kingpin an keep Pop Diva safe from this guy. Only time will tell.

## Bobby Cinema Movie idea# 3:

### Pitching my to movie studios

### Genre: Action and Comedy

### Ages: 15-35

### Movie idea:

### Robin and Lester S.V.U.:

Lester Willis is a P.I. who works as an consultant in St. Louis P.D. He has a new partner on a case that he's assigned to from his boss who is the mayor of St. Louis where his consultant job is his bread and butter that he supports himself with. He is partnered to help with this case Robin Muster. An attractive female tough police officer who foiled a bank heist as posing

as a hostage. Robin doesn't want a partner or some outsider from the force helping on this case. Since she doesn't know what this case is about. Mostly Robin is a loner and doesn't trust anybody, ever since was raped in college. She became a cop, so she find this rapist and take him out as her vendetta. The mayor assigned her to S.V.U. special victims unit and promote her to detective sergeant. The mayor picked her to partner up with Lester, it might be the same rapist who raped her in college. Lester with his excellent detective skills and Robin's police instincts and might identify the serial rapist. Mostly Robin hasn't told the mayor, she doesn't know who this guy is because he was a wearing a mask. Robin is reluctant to partner up with Lester, she has no choice she wants to go after this guy. So, they start teaming up and trying to find this guy. They use the city hall computer room where they can work and to track down this killer. They figure out this serial rapist owns a pharmaceutical company and creates illegal date rape drugs on the side to sell it to top frat guys. To have sex with girls that are

unconscious. These frat guys were interns in pharmaceutical company. They were never connected to this company, since they never ratted out who send them the date rape drugs. This serial date rapist works slipping roofies in their drinks. They get unconscious and get raped at the same time. This rapist drugs them and rape them all at once. This rapist is a date rape drug kingpin, who selling date rape drugs to terrorist. Who are planning use the date rape drug in syringe and get them shots to put them unconscious so they can steal anything in sight. They got one week track down this Serial Rape drug kingpin before he sells his drugs to terrorist. Robin not only trying to save this victims who were about to be raped by this guy, she wants to exact her revenge on this bastard who raped her. I just hope Robin doesn't go to far in her vendetta of her and not cross any lines. Can these two find this rapist and bring this man to justice. Only time will tell.

**Bobby Cinema Movie idea# 4:**

**Pitching my movie to Movie Studios**

**Genre: Action and Superhero**

**Ages: 18-35**

Mr. Stealth: Robbie Travis as an eighteen year old teenager he was being pushed around ever since he has a kid, lead by Monty Hewitt. A rich popular jock who is the captain of football and basketball team. Monty popularity isn't just in sports and wealth, he was dating Chelsea Allen whose family is second richest girl in Allen City whose family was the founder of the city in 1870 Abraham Allen. Allen City Ohio is a second big city and twenty miles from Cleveland. Right now, the city is on a major crime wave. Robbie is friends with Chelsea's

brother Abe Allen IV and his family Allen industries is worth 50 billion dollars where they're famous Allen chocolate bars and high tech technology they build for the military. Robbie encountered Monty again, when he looked at Chelsea and starts grinning. Monty saw that and doesn't like geeks like Robbie looking at Chelsea for a minute. Guys like Robbie don't get girls like Chelsea. Monty beats him up and after the fight was over, he didn't come to school all week after being humiliated by Monty. Luckily for him, his parents are out of town for a couple weeks. Robbie thought about, taking his GED and go to college early. So, he hasn't have to deal with Monty and his posse Allen City High. Fate changes when Abe and Chelsea came over and Chelsea apologizes to Robbie about Monty's behavior. He asked him to leave him alone, but I don't think Monty will leave him alone. Robbie understood, he wishes he can get back Monty for one day for all the torture he did to people like Robbie. Abe already fixed that problem and ask him go to R&D department in an hour, he wants to

show him something. Robbie is a little about reluctant what Abe wants to show him. But he decide, take a look and see what he wants to show him. Abe and Chelsea shows him a pair of sunglasses that R&D department built for the military. But it was never tested out or went into production. Robbie ask what this sunglasses do. Chelsea told him, they don't know. But they are worried if it goes in the wrong hands. So, they ask him to guard these glasses with his life. They don't want these glasses in the wrong hands. Robbie goes along with it and puts them in his pocket. Robbie asked him if they want go to a movie, they said yes. After the movie, they're were a couple of muggers pulling a gun on them and ask them for money now. They were about give them the money, until they ask for the sun glasses and the mugger was about to shoot Robbie until he put the glasses close circuit his body and disappeared. The glasses made him invisible, not only that it also made him strong, super fast, shape shift, leap really high, make him highly intelligent and teleport anywhere to punch out the mugger when he

teleported from the alley. Robbie, Chelsea and Abe decided these glasses can use for a good purpose. The crime is really high in this city and we can use these glasses to rid the world of crime. With their ally who somebody trust is their older brother John who is elected D.A. trying to put Monty's father Rupert who is a top drug lord against for drug dealing and murder in Allen City. He is the one gave him a police scanner and give him information on the guys John is trying to put away. They know they can let these glasses get in the wrong hands from Monty and his father. Together all four of these guys trying to give people hope Allen City and make a difference in the world. Can Robbie be with Chelsea and rid the world of crime in this city at the same time. Only time will tell.

## About the Author

Bobby Cinema is autistic. His family is from India, and he is the first member of his family who was born in America. He graduated in Maryville High School in 1998 and graduated from college at Northwest Missouri State University in 2004. He lived in Los Angeles for three years trying to sell his movie in the big screen. He had an eight-year struggle trying to sell his movie and his book. But he has been rejected for a long time. He wrote this book and dedicates this for his niece Lakeh Chavala. Sylvester Stallone is his hero, who aspired to be a screenwriter when he took a chance to write Rocky. Bobby wrote twenty movie scripts and three books. This is his first book to be out in the bookstores.